W9-ATO-626

MORE THAN SUNNY

SHELLEY JOHANNES

Abrams Books for Young Readers
New York

OR...

it's
SUNNY
AND
BiRDY!

it's
SUNNY...

AND STUCK.

BUT MAYBE . . .

WE'RE
IN LUCK?

NOW SOGGY
AND DOGGY!

it's WINDY AND
SQUIRRELLY!

WiNTER...

AND waity.

BUT I'M WARM AND SOCKSY.

LET'S BE SNOWY AND FOXY!

SHHH...

it's SNOWY
AND DOEY.

ARE YOU READY AND SLEDDY?!

WELL, it's LATE AND SHOVELY.

or it's LATE... AND LOVELY.

it's
BEDtiME...

WHO COULD it BE?

To Matthew—
who first paired sunny with birdy,
and windy with squirrelly,
and always sees more

More than thank you to Emma Ledbetter, Stephen Barr, Ann Bobco, and Heather Kelly.

The illustrations in this book were made with pencil and mixed media on tracing paper and finished digitally.

Library of Congress Cataloging-in-Publication Data
Names: Johannes, Shelley, author, illustrator. Title: More than sunny / by Shelley Johannes.
Description: New York : Abrams Books for Young Readers, [2021] | Summary:
Throughout the year, a brother and sister, and sometimes their parents, enjoy weather that is
sunny and birdy, rainy and wormy, windy and squirrelly, or snowy and doey.
Identifiers: LCCN 2020006072 | ISBN 9781419741814 (hardcover)
Subjects: CYAC: Stories in rhyme. | Seasons--Fiction. | Weather--Fiction. |
Brothers and sisters--Fiction. | Family life--Fiction.
Classification: LCC PZ8.3.J613 Mor 2021 | DDC [E]--dc23
LC record available at https://lccn.loc.gov/2020006072

Text and illustrations copyright © 2021 Shelley Johannes
Book design by Heather Kelly

Published in 2021 by Abrams Books for Young Readers, an imprint of ABRAMS.
All rights reserved. No portion of this book may be reproduced, stored in a retrieval system,
or transmitted in any form or by any means, mechanical, electronic, photocopying, recording,
or otherwise, without written permission from the publisher.

Printed and bound in China
10 9 8 7 6 5 4 3 2 1

Abrams Books for Young Readers are available at special discounts when purchased in
quantity for premiums and promotions as well as fundraising or educational use. Special editions can also be
created to specification. For details, contact specialsales@abramsbooks.com or the address below.

Abrams® is a registered trademark of Harry N. Abrams, Inc.

ABRAMS The Art of Books
195 Broadway, New York, NY 10007
abramsbooks.com

FREDERICK COUNTY PUBLIC LIBRARIES

SEP   2021

FREDERICK COUNTY PUBLIC LIBRARIES

SEP   2021